STORY OF A
Tree

DIANE BARRETT

ISBN 978-1-64079-280-7 (paperback)
ISBN 978-1-64079-281-4 (digital)

Christian Faith Publishing, Inc.
832 Park Avenue
Meadville, PA 16335
www.christianfaithpublishing.com

Printed in the United States of America

I dedicate *Story of a Tree* to my precious grandchildren, Jackson, Cosette, Lydia, Graham and Lily with love. Since the day you were born, I have continued praying for you, asking God to fill you with spiritual wisdom and understanding. Then you will live the kind of life that honors and pleases the Lord in every way. You will produce every kind of good fruit as you grow and learn to know God better. In my prayers, I am always thanking God for you!

It's all true, everything happened just like my Father God said! The beginning to the end! God came down from heaven in the clouds with his newly created city and now I live happily with him forever!

The city is more beautiful than I could have ever imagined. It's made of pure gold that shimmers like a very precious jewel. I like to walk right down the middle of the golden streets that are clear as glass to the center of the city toward my Father's throne. He's seated there with my friend Jesus at his right side. He invites me to climb up and sit with him in the highest seat in heaven, right next to Jesus, as he tells me all the secrets of heaven and explains every mystery. Then I climb down and run to our special place under the tree. It's not just any tree—it's the tree of life! My Father planted it on both sides of the crystal-bright river of life that flows straight out of his throne. The tree of life grows a different kind of sweet fruit to bite into every month.

When I arrive to sit under the branches of the tree of life, he's waiting there just for me! I laugh in my belly and run to his lap. He scoops me up, holding me tight! As I look at his bright shining face and into his eyes that sparkle like flames of fire, I say, "Father, tell me again the story of how I got here! Tell me our favorite story, the *Story of a Tree*!"

Father replied, "Long before the mountains were born, long before I gave birth to the earth, from once upon a time to kingdom come, I am God!

"Long ago, even before I made the world, I had you in mind. I had settled on you as the focus of my love. I knew you inside and out, every bone in your body. I knew exactly how I would make you. How I would sculpt you from nothing into something. I saw all the days of your life before you lived even one day!

"And so, this is how the story of you with me began…"

* * *

I created the heavens and the earth. At first, the earth was formless, empty and dark. And then I began to speak into existence all that I created.

On the first day, I said, "Let there be light!" And there was light. I separated the light from the darkness, calling the light day and darkness night.

I created an expanse on the second day, and it separated the waters of heaven from the waters of earth, and I called it sky.

And then, on the third day, I created the dry ground by gathering the waters, calling the dry ground land and the gathered waters seas.

I also created vegetation, all sorts of plants and trees with seed-bearing fruit.

Then on the fourth day, I created the sun, moon, and the stars to give light to the earth and to separate the day and the night.

On the fifth day, I created every living creature of the seas and every winged bird, blessing them to multiply and fill the waters and the sky with life.

The sixth day, I created animals to fill the earth—wild animals, tame animals, and all the small crawling animals.

I also created man and woman. I said to my Son Jesus and the Holy Spirit, "Let us make man in our image, according to our likeness, for our pleasure."

I blessed them and said, "Have lots of children so that there will be many of you to fill the earth."

I finished the work of my creation on the seventh day, and so I rested, blessing it and making it holy.

I looked over everything I had made, and it was so very good!

On the day I created man, I took dust from the ground and formed man from it. I breathed the breath of life into the man's nostrils, and the man became a living person.

I crowned him with glory and honor. I blessed him and put him in charge of everything I made, placing him over all my creation.

With the breath in his lungs, he joined the mountains and hills as they burst into song. The earth and all the trees shouted my praise!

Then I planted a garden, and there I placed the man I had made to tend and watch over it. I made all sorts of trees grow up from the ground—trees that were beautiful and that produced delicious fruit.

In the middle of the garden I placed the tree that gives life and the tree that gives the knowledge of good and evil. A river flowed from the land, watering the garden.

The tree of life is the symbol of my provision for eternal life—the highest life, the best life, the greatest joys, and the most fulfilled life. This tree is the symbol of unbelievable, glorious life without death.

My plan for you all along was for you to live with me forever. I commanded the man, "You may eat the fruit from any tree in the garden. But you must not eat the fruit from the tree which gives the knowledge of good and evil. If you ever eat from that tree, you will be separated from me and you will die!"

Then I said, "It's not good for the man to be alone. I will make him a helper who is just right for him." So I caused the man to fall into a deep sleep. And while he was sleeping, I took a rib from his side and used the rib to make a woman. Then I brought her to the man, and I walked with them in the garden in the cool of the day among the trees.

However, the man and the woman did not obey my command, and they ate fruit from the tree of the knowledge of good and evil. Just as I had warned, sin came into the world and separated us. And with sin, death was just a matter of time.

Then I said to my Son Jesus and the Holy Spirit, "Look, the man and the woman have become like us, knowing good and evil. What if they reach out, take fruit from the tree of life, and eat it? Then they will live apart from me forever!"

And so, because of how much I love you and planned for you to live with me forever, I had to remove them from the garden.

After sending them out, I stationed angels to the east of the garden. I placed a flaming sword that flashed back and forth to guard the path to the tree of life so they would no longer have access to it.

If they ate from the tree of life, you would live apart from me forever in a sinful state with its results— sadness, crying and pain— with no hope of relief.

I loved you too much to let that happen!

Long before the creation of the world, I had plans for another tree. It would be on that tree that you would get back the life that was lost because of sin so that you would have access to the tree of life and live with me forever.

At just the right time, I sent my Son Jesus Christ to earth, where he laid down his perfect life for you. He bore your sins in his own body on the tree. Jesus himself died for you to pay for your sins.

He never sinned, but he died to bring you safely home to me. He bled and then he died and then he rose again so that you might die to sin and live for righteousness.

I always knew I was going to do this for you and for all who accepted him. For to those who believed in him, he gave the right to become my children. All you needed to do was to trust him to save you.

I wanted everyone to choose my Son who died on the tree in the middle. I wanted everyone to live with me forever, but not everyone chose him. Some rejected him!

But you chose the sacrifice of my Son on the tree in the middle, and you get to eat the fruit from the tree of life and live with me forever!

Then I asked you to do something very courageous! I asked you to trust me!

Just like the tree of life was in the center of the garden with the man and the woman, I asked you to put me in the center of your life, until I come and get you to bring you home, where you will eat from the tree of life for all eternity.

I never wanted you to live like those who are cursed, who put their trust in humans, who rely on their own strength and turn their hearts away from me.

They are like the tumbleweed, a bush with no roots in the desert, with no hope for their future. They live in the dry wilderness, where nothing can grow.

But the ones who put their trust in me are blessed! I asked you to delight in my law. To meditate on it day and night, to believe, to trust and rely on me. Put your hope and confident expectation in me!

When you trusted me and put me in the center of your life, your life became like a tree planted along a riverbank, with roots that grow strong and deep into the water.

Like a tree that's not afraid when hot weather comes, because its leaves never dry up, they stay beautiful and are always green.

So it has no worries when there is no rain. It keeps on bearing fruit and is successful in everything it does.

And I promised you, the one who wins the victory will have the right to eat the fruit from the tree of life that is in my garden in paradise.

So at just the right time, I said to my Son Jesus, "Go back to earth and gather my children, the ones who won the victory through believing in me and putting me at the center of their lives, the ones who trusted me and relied on me until the very end."

Now you are here with me in paradise! I wiped away every tear from your eye. There's no more death, sadness, crying, or pain. All of that is gone forever. I made everything new!

There will never be night again! The city doesn't need the sun or the moon to shine on it because my glory is its light! Now you can drink freely of the water of life, eat the fruit from the tree of life, and live with me forever and ever and ever!

ABOUT THE AUTHOR

Diane Barrett is passionate about God and his Word! Through years of ministry she's taught children, teens, and adults to understand who God is through his Word and grow in their faith. As a speaker, mentor, and counselor, Diane loves to encourage and challenge individuals to respond to God's loving plan for their lives and discover the pleasure of life with God rooted in the Bible. Diane has been married to her husband Tim since 1977, and they have two daughters and five grandchildren. She lives in Northern California where she invests time with her family, serving on staff at her church, and training the next generation of Christian leaders.

CPSIA information can be obtained
at www.ICGtesting.com
Printed in the USA
BVHW022222101118
532611BV00003B/5/P

9 781640 792807